HOPEFULL
HOPEFULL
WHEN YOU FALL ASLEEP...

by Joshua Eastvold

HOPEFULLY, HOPEFULLY,
WHEN YOU FALL ASLEEP,
YOU DON'T SEE A

GIRAFFE

BUT IF YOU DO,
JUST GIVE OUT
A LOUD

LAUGH

HOPEFULLY, HOPEFULLY, WHEN YOU FALL ASLEEP, YOU DON'T SEE A

SHARK

BUT YOU MIGHT
WANT TO LOOK
FOR A FIN
IN THE

DARK

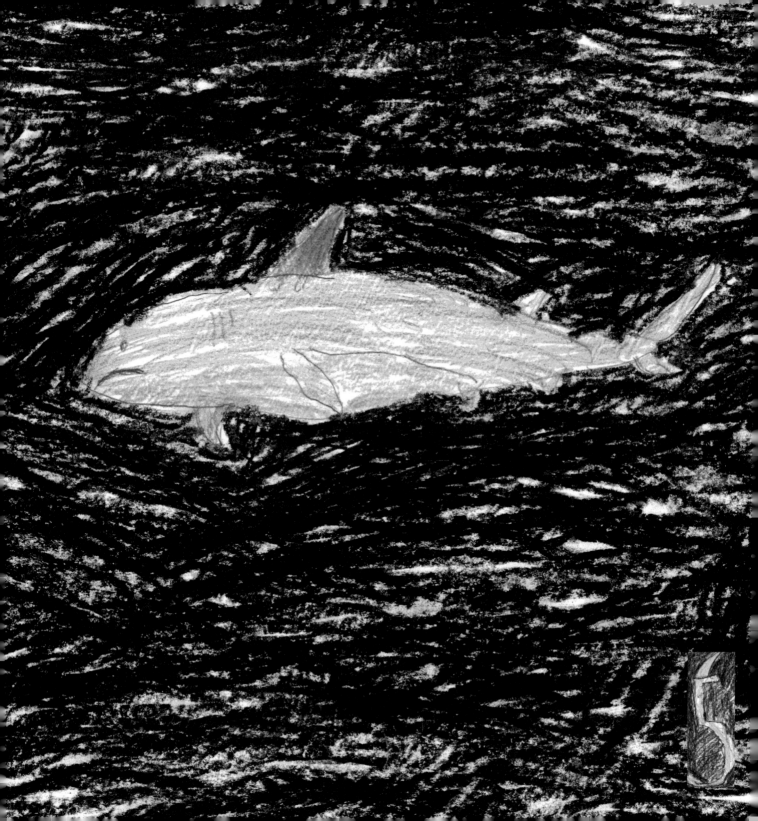

HOPEFULLY, HOPEFULLY,
WHEN YOU FALL ASLEEP,
YOU DON'T SEE AN

ELEPHANT

BUT IF YOU DON'T
SPOT ONE,
MAYBE IT ALREADY

CAME AND WENT

HOPEFULLY, HOPEFULLY,
WHEN YOU FALL ASLEEP,
YOU DON'T SEE A

GRIZZLY BEAR

BUT YOU MIGHT
WANT TO CHECK

OVER THERE

↳→

HOPEFULLY, HOPEFULLY,
WHEN YOU FALL ASLEEP,
YOU DON'T SEE A

REINDEER

BUT YOU MIGHT
WANT TO CHECK

HOPEFULLY, HOPEFULLY,
WHEN YOU FALL ASLEEP,
YOU DON'T SEE A

CROCODILE

BUT YOU MIGHT
WANT TO CHECK
UNDER THE BED EVERY

ONCE IN A WHILE

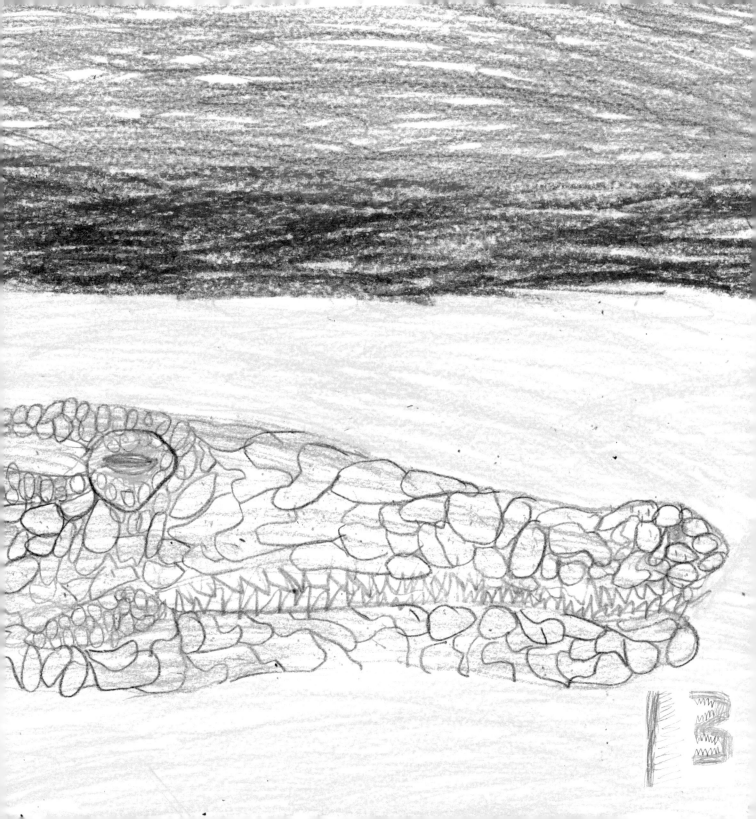

HOPEFULLY, HOPEFULLY,
WHEN YOU FALL ASLEEP,
YOU DON'T SEE AN

ARMADILLO

BUT YOU MIGHT
WANT TO CHECK

UNDER YOUR

PILLOW

HOPEFULLY, HOPEFULLY,
WHEN YOU FALL ASLEEP,
YOU DON'T SEE A

SNAKE

BUT YOU MIGHT
WANT TO CHECK TWICE
TO AVOID A BIG

MISTAKE

HOPEFULLY, HOPEFULLY,
WHEN YOU FALL ASLEEP,
YOU DON'T SEE A

CROW

BUT IN THE DARK,
HOW COULD YOU

KNOW

HOPEFULLY, HOPEFULLY,
WHEN YOU FALL ASLEEP,
YOU DON'T SEE A

CAT

BUT UP ON THE
WINDOW SILL
IS WHERE IT

WOULD BE AT

HOPEFULLY, HOPEFULLY,
WHEN YOU FALL ASLEEP,
YOU DON'T SEE A

RACCOON

BUT DON'T WORRY,
THEY USUALLY
SLEEP UNTIL

NOON

HOPEFULLY, HOPEFULLY,
WHEN YOU FALL ASLEEP,
YOU DON'T SEE AN

ALLIGATOR

BUT YOU MIGHT
WANT TO CHECK
IN THE

CORNER LATER

HOPEFULLY, HOPEFULLY,
WHEN YOU FALL ASLEEP,
YOU DON'T SEE A

KANGAROO

BUT I'LL GIVE YOU A

CLUE

SHE'S STUCK IN SOME

GLUE

HOPEFULLY, HOPEFULLY,
WHEN YOU FALL ASLEEP,
YOU DON'T SEE A

SEAL

BUT IF YOU DO,
THAT'S NOT A
BIG

DEAL

HOPEFULLY, HOPEFULLY,
WHEN YOU FALL ASLEEP,
YOU DON'T SEE A

LION

BUT IF YOU DO,
HE'S PROBABLY ALL
ALONE AND

CRYIN'

31

HOPEFULLY, HOPEFULLY,
ALL YOU SEE
IS THE

MOON

SO CLOSE YOUR EYES,
AND GO TO SLEEP
SOON

32

78807200R00020

Made in the USA
Lexington, KY
13 January 2018